DISCARD

6 1158
LIC LIBRARY

D1311775

The truth about Santa Claus

DISCARD

$19.95
ocn173986334
12/10/2007

THE · TRUTH · ABOUT
Santa · Claus

THE · TRUTH · ABOUT
Santa · Claus

COMPILED BY
THE BLUE LANTERN STUDIO

GREEN TIGER PRESS
MMVII

COPYRIGHT © 2007 LAUGHING ELEPHANT

ALL RIGHTS RESERVED   FIRST PRINTING   PRINTED IN CHINA

ISBN 978-1-59583-187-3

GREEN TIGER PRESS

A DIVISION OF LAUGHING ELEPHANT

WWW.LAUGHINGELEPHANT.COM

Santa is sometimes shown
as a very small man,

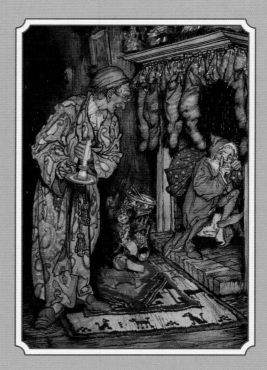

But he is overwhelmingly pictured as large,
bulky and magnificent.
Always he has a beard,
always it is white, as befits his great age.

Santa occasionally seems sly — a man with many
secrets. He sometimes lays his finger
beside his nose to say that he knows
all that we know, and more.

He almost always seems wise and good. Most
frequently he smiles –
a smile from a profound happiness,
a smile of infinite charity.

Santa Claus wears heavy, fur-edged garments.
The cloth is usually red, but as you can see here,
that is not his only choice.

The largest truth about Santa Claus
is that he is kind.

He wants to give whatever makes people happy,
and he spends his whole life doing it.

He spends the entire year
preparing for Christmas,
and then makes the superhuman effort
to give to every child.

Santa does have near-human weaknesses.
He loves to smoke – usually a pipe,
but on occasion a cigar. He loves wine,
and good food, especially sweets.

He is always glad to meet new friends,
and enjoys sharing a glass of champagne
or a plum pudding with them.

Everyone knows that Santa Claus lives
at the North Pole with many elves who help
him with his incredible tasks, and who are also
friends and playmates.

It is less known that angels are also
his constant companions, friends and helpers.

Mrs. Claus is, of course,
Santa's most constant companion and
confidante, though she never accompanies him
on his Christmas journey around the world.

Santa loves his reindeer. They live outside all
year because they do not enjoy the warmth of
his dwelling. Some people believe Comet is his
favorite. We believe he loves them all equally.

In preparing for his Christmas visit
to the children of the world Santa first reads
all the letters he receives during the year.
Next he meets with his fairy friends,
for fairies go everywhere and hear what
people say, so they are a fine source for the
kind of things he needs to know.

After gathering all this information
Santa organizes it into a completed plan
of action and, with all his helpers,
brings it to reality.

Santa is a maker as well as a giver.
Though the elves help him make his
toys, he understands every process and
frequently does the work himself. Painting is
one task at which he is especially adroit.

He feels joy in the planning,
in the making,
and, of course, in the giving
of the products of his workshop.

The aspect of Santa Claus which is
most difficult for us to comprehend is that
he can do so much in so short a time;
that he can travel so far and so quickly;

that he can make and carry so much.
— Magic is clearly the answer,
and this we can never understand;
only be grateful for its power in our lives.

Almost always Santa uses a sleigh drawn by reindeer, but we have reports that on occasion, for reasons we don't understand, he has used other means of transport.

As to be expected, Santa needs help for his Christmas deliveries. Elves and angels are the usual helpers, but on rare occasions, the toys which he is delivering come to life and help out.

24

Santa Claus and his reindeer usually land on the roof of the house he is visiting. If it has a chimney, which is his strong preference, he descends it and places his gifts.

How he gets up and down the chimney,
particularly when a fire is burning,
is another mystery, explained only by his
magical powers.

When there is no chimney Santa must enter
homes by window or door.

When inside he works silently,
placing his presents, filling children's
stockings, sometimes adding decorative touches
to Christmas trees. If there is a snack,
he enjoys it. Even though his night is so long
and his task so huge,
he does everything carefully.

Sometimes, even with all his unimaginable strength, Santa falls asleep at his tasks. His helpers try to wake him, but it is so comfortable in a warm home.

When this happens Santa is liable to be
caught, to be encountered by excited children.
When Santa does meet with children he is not
chagrined, but delighted, for love of children
fills his life. He stays to play with them, to find
out what they think and feel.

He gets to know better some of the children
to whom he has devoted his life.
These rare accidents are one of the happiest
moments in the life of Santa Claus.

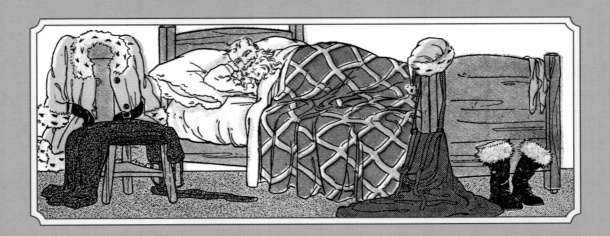

When Christmas night is over, Santa, even
though a magical being without most of the
weaknesses of humans, is exhausted. First he
takes a long, long nap. Then he takes a
vacation, usually to a warm place, sometimes
with a beach. Then returns home, and takes up
the task of planning to make the children of the
world a little happier.

PICTURE CREDITS

COVER	N.C. WYETH. "OLE ST. NICK," 1925.
ENDPAPERS	UNKNOWN. FROM *THE NIGHT BEFORE CHRISTMAS*, C.1896
HALF TITLE	THOMAS NAST. DRAWING, C. 1890.
FRONTISPIECE	UNKNOWN. FROM *THE NIGHT BEFORE CHRISTMAS*, C. 1896.
TITLE PAGE	UNKNOWN. MAGAZINE COVER, C. 1920.
COPYRIGHT	GERTRUD AND WALTHER CASPARI.
	FROM *KINDERLAND, DU ZAUBERLAND*, 1908.
2	UPPER: UNKNOWN. FROM *SANTA CLAUS AND HIS WORKS*, N.D.
	LOWER LEFT: UNKNOWN. FROM *THE NIGHT BEFORE CHRISTMAS*, C. 1917.
	LOWER RIGHT: ARTHUR RACKHAM. FROM *THE NIGHT BEFORE CHRISTMAS*, 1931.
3	MAGINEL WRIGHT BARNEY. MAGAZINE COVER, 1938.
4	UPPER: UNKNOWN. POSTCARD, C. 1910.
	LOWER LEFT: JOSEPH CUMMINGS CHASE. FROM *THE NIGHT BEFORE CHRISTMAS*, 1913
	LOWER: UNKNOWN. POSTCARD, N.D.
5	UPPER: THOMAS NAST. "SANTA CLAUS," C. 1890.
	LOWER LEFT: UNKNOWN. POSTCARD, C. 1909.
	LOWER RIGHT: UNKNOWN. POSTCARD, C. 1931.
6	UPPER: UNKNOWN. POSTCARD, N.D.
	LOWER: UNKNOWN. POSTCARD, N.D.
7	UPPER LEFT: UNKNOWN. POSTCARD, N.D.
	UPPER RIGHT: UNKNOWN. POSTCARD, C. 1909.
	LOWER LEFT: UNKNOWN. POSTCARD, N.D.
	LOWER RIGHT: UNKNOWN. POSTCARD, N.D.
8	HOWARD A. TERPNING. " 'TWAS THE NIGHT BEFORE CHRISTMAS," N.D.
9	UPPER: UNKNOWN. POSTCARD, C. 1916.
	LOWER: UNKNOWN. POSTCARD, C. 1917.
10	UPPER: UNKNOWN. POSTCARD, N.D.
	LOWER LEFT: UNKNOWN. POSTCARD, C. 1916.
	LOWER RIGHT: UNKNOWN. POSTCARD, C. 1916.
11	UPPER: UNKNOWN. POSTCARD, N.D.
	LOWER LEFT: UNKNOWN. ADVERTISEMENT, C. 1915.
	LOWER RIGHT: UNKNOWN. POSTCARD, N.D.
12	UPPER: UNKNOWN. POSTCARD, C. 1922.
	LOWER: E. BOYD SMITH. FROM *SANTA CLAUS AND ALL ABOUT HIM*, 1908.
13	UPPER: LORE FRIEDRICH. FROM *ALLE JAHRE WIEDER*, C. 1930.
	LOWER LEFT: UNKNOWN. POSTCARD, N.D.
	LOWER RIGHT: UNKNOWN. POSTCARD, C. 1906.
14	UNKNOWN. ADVERTISEMENT, 1952.
15	UPPER: JOHN RAE. *THE THREE LITTLE FROGS*, 1924
	LOWER: KEITH WARD. MAGAZINE COVER, 1931.
16	UPPER: E. BOYD SMITH. FROM *SANTA CLAUS AND ALL ABOUT HIM*, 1908.
	LOWER: CORINNE PAULI WATERALL. FROM *AT PLAY*, 1940.
17	JOHN DUKES MCKEE. MAGAZINE ILLUSTRATION, 1932.
18	RICHARD ANDRE. "SANTA CLAUS IN HIS WORKSHOP," 1895.
19	J.C. LEYENDECKER. MAGAZINE COVER, 1920.
20	MAURICE LELOIR. MAGAZINE ILLUSTRATION, 1910.
21	N.C. WYETH. "OLE ST. NICK," 1925.
22	UPPER: CEFISCHER (CARL E. FISCHER). POSTCARD, N.D.
	MIDDLE: FRANK VER BECK.
	FROM *VER BECK'S BEARS IN MOTHER GOOSE-LAND*, C. 1910.
	LOWER: UNKNOWN. POSTCARD, C. 1910.

PICTURE CREDITS